Good Night Pillow Fight

By Sally Cook
Illustrated by Laura Cornell

JOANNA COTLER BOOKS
An Imprint of HarperCollinsPublishers

Sweet dreams and many thanks to Justin Chanda, Melissa Zuckerman,
Alicia Mikles, Ruiko Tokunaga, Jason Britton, Liz and Alex Cook, and Mom
—S.C.

Likewise, to those who make my miracles
—L.C.

Good Night Pillow Fight
Text copyright © 2004 by Sally Cook   Illustrations copyright © 2004 by Laura Cornell
Printed in the U.S.A.   All rights reserved.   www.harperchildrens.com
Library of Congress Cataloging-in-Publication Data   Cook, Sally.   Good night pillow fight © by Sally Cook ;
illustrated by Laura Cornell.— 1st ed.   p. cm.   Summary: A city full of parents tries to get their children to go to sleep,
while the children insist on playing games.   ISBN 0-06-205189-X — ISBN 0-06-205190-3 (lib. bdg.)   [1. Bedtime—Fiction. 2. Parents
and children—Fiction. 3. Stories in rhyme.]   I. Cornell, Laura, ill. II. Title.   PZ8.3.C7694Go 2004   2003008933   [E]—dc21
Typography by Alicia Mikles   1 2 3 4 5 6 7 8 9 10   ❖   First Edition

To Laura Cornell, Joanna Cotler,
Holly McGhee and Kate McMullan: four greats

—S.C.

To Lilly, always, and my pal Sally

—L.C.

Good

night.

Pillow

fight!

Kiss

my cheek.

Hide

and seek!

Lights out

now!

I'M WAY

YO

RNING
U!

Peek-a-boo!

No more
juice!

Jack Sprat . . .

Not that!

Three Bears?

Who cares?

This one?

GO TO

BED!

YOU HAVEN'T

READ!

Let's count sheep.

I can't sleep.

One,

two,

Give it a try.

three,

Why should I?

four,

five, six, seven, eight . . .

Are there lots more?

Isn't it getting late?

So many sheep...

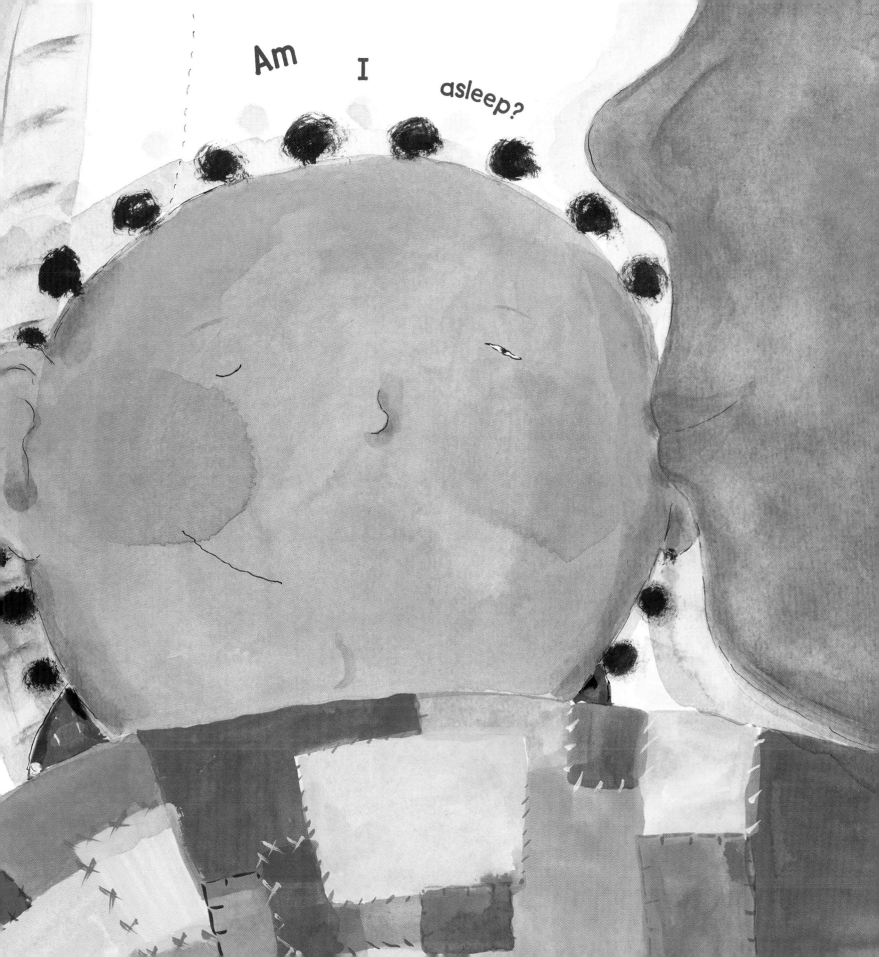

Off with the light.

Good night.